Two of Everything

Babette Cole

RED FOX

Demetrius and Paula Ogglebutt were
two perfectly beautiful children...

but...

they had two problem parents who could never agree about anything.

Their opinions were never the same about anything.

Dad's idea of a holiday.

Dad's idea of a dog. →

Dad's idea of art.

The longer Mr and Mrs Ogglebutt lived together,
the more they disliked each other.

They had started off as quite good-looking parents.

But because they had ugly thoughts about each other...
it began to show and they became uglier and uglier.

They started playing tricks on each other:
Mr Ogglebutt put concrete powder in his
wife's bath salts!

She put fireworks in his bangers and mash!

To get his own back he buried wrigglers in her mud pack!

Then she hid a present from one of his cows in his cap!

And he boiled her underwear until her knickers shrank!

Paula and Demetrius became worried by their parents'
behaviour. They thought it might be their fault.

They were very sad and confused.

They decided to see if anyone else at their school had the same problem.

Loads of kids turned up! The result of the meeting was that it is not the fault of the children if their parents behave like five-year-olds.

"What do we do about it?" said Demetrius.
"I've got an idea," said Paula.

So they went to see the vicar to ask if he could 'un-marry' their parents.

"What a cracking idea," said the vicar. "You know it might be the only thing they will ever agree about!"

"Brilliant!" said their parents.
"Why didn't we think of that?"

"Because you are always
arguing," said Paula and
Demetrius.

They had lots of
things to organise...

like sending out the
'un-wedding' invitations

and ordering the
'un-wedding' cake.

The 'un-wedding' was a joyous occasion for everyone.

Once their parents had jetted off on their separate 'un-honeymoons'...

Demetrius and Paula bulldozed the house as an 'un-wedding' present.

In its place they built two separate houses. One to suit each parent.

These were connected by a secret tunnel only big enough for Demetrius and Paula.

And, of course, because they now lived in two houses,
they ordered two of everything they wanted.

They also ended up with two very
contented parents who could
live happily ever after – apart.

With thanks to Ron and Atie

The End

A Red Fox Book
Published by Random House Children's Books 61-63 Uxbridge Road, London W5 5SA
Copyright © Babette Cole 1997
9 10
First published in Great Britain by The Bodley Head Children's Books 2000
This Red Fox edition 2001
All rights reserved
Printed in Singapore by Tien Wah Press (PTE) Ltd
THE RANDOM HOUSE GROUP Limited Reg. No. 954009
www.kidsatrandomhouse.co.uk
Addresses for companies within The Random House Group Limited can be found
at: www.randomhouse.co.uk/offices.htm

ISBN 13 : 9780099220626